Dream Garden

Tales of Flowers and Butterflies

by Ernst Kreidolf

A Star & Elephant Book

Translation
by
Elaine Boney   Silke Reavis
&
The Green Tiger Editorial Staff

The pictures herein are reproduced from the original watercolors
by Ernst Kreidolf

Original Title: Der Traumgarten
Copyright 1976 by Rotapfel Verlag AG Zurich
First American Edition, published by arrangement with Rotapfel Verlag
ISBN 0-914676-10-5   Paper over board

A Star & Elephant Book
from
THE GREEN TIGER PRESS
7458 La Jolla Blvd.
La Jolla, California 92037

Dream Garden

Invitation to Dance

The Butterfly Ladies sat in a garden of parsley. Their wings were silken gowns and satin robes. They wore hats with feathers and fine shoes.

Then there came Beetle Knights in armor and coats of mail; but instead of bearing shield and spear, they bore posies, for they had come not as warriors but as dancing partners.

"May I have the honor, Miss Wood Nymph?" said green Ground Beetle and made a bow.

"May I venture to ask for a dance?" asked Tiger Beetle of Miss Checkerspot.

"May I prostrate myself at your feet?" said Dung Beetle to Spanish Flag, Aurora, and Miss Blue Argus all at the same time, so that no one knew which one he meant.

The May Beetle, however, handed Miss Lemon Leaf a sweet bouquet of raspberries and said, "I kiss your hand, gracious damsel."

The Butterfly Ladies were delighted with the compliments and answered:
> "We welcome you, ye Knights so bold,
> With armor of emerald, copper, and gold.
> You are so well-mannered and refined,
> To dance with you, we are much inclined."

Then they rose, the Beetles offered each an arm, and the dance began.

The Knight With the Magic Wand

Once upon a summer time
Appeared a goodly knight.
He happened from a distant clime,
And what was his delight?

He held in hand a magic wand
That glittered, star on star.
Where was this wondrous blossom found?
The rumor spread afar.

Gently he shook his floral staff.
They watched him with amaze.
Therefrom as many stars flew off
As all his living days.

If on one flower a star fell down
When the wand waved above,
The blooming ceased; this flower was gone,
Sunk wilted to its grave.

At this how grieved were all those flowers!
Many were sore afraid
To find their bloom was but for hours
They'd thought could never fade.

The knight had come and gone away,
Passing from green to green,
Always keeping his magic sway
And scattering starlets between.

Swallow Tail

Sir Swallow Tail lived in a green park with his daughters. The Dear Lady lay in the hammock, had the Wood Nymph fan her, and said, "Tell me a story."

Wood Nymph began: "Once upon a time, there were little caterpillars who lived in the carrot tops. When they grew up, they wanted more beautiful clothes so they shed their garments of green and received in their place new clothes with many yellow circles and black polka-dots. When they grew still larger, they wanted to be dressed even more beautifully; they shed their clothing again and received clothes with black rings and red polka-dots. When they were quite grown up and there were no clothes more beautiful than the ones they had, they said to each other: 'It is tiring and boring always to have to crawl — if only we could fly!' They climbed way up high and spun a button of silk from which they twirled a silver thread. 'It's going to happen!' they said. The next day, they no longer looked like caterpillars but like long faces waiting for something. They had become pupae and had to swing in a chrysalis for many days, without anything to eat or drink. But suddenly the golden shell split apart and splendid butterflies with long pointed wings came out. They could fly like swallows; they were Swallowtails."

"How pretty! How charming!" cried the Dear Lady and clapped her hands. "Honey-bee, bring us some honey! Telling the story has made Wood Nymph very thirsty."

Then Sir Swallow Tail came back from the hunt. He sat in the green park beside the honey jar with his daughters and Wood Nymph had to tell the story all over again.

Miss Fennel in Green

Maiden in green,
Whispers unseen,
Starry blue crown
Veiled by her gown.
"O, would I were a bride in white,
'Twere all my joy and my delight.
But must I, to my despair,
Linger, hid in this green hair."

"Master Wallflower,
There you are,
In a frock coat
And a copper hat!
Money in sack,
Nothing you lack.
Man of the Hour,
Master Wallflower!

No girl rich enough
For this stingy stuff.
He's for Wallflower only,
Tight hand on his money."

Now Mr. Phlox comes down the lane,
And in his hand a silver cane.
"Charming specimen!
Take him, he's not mine.
Always swinging a cane,
Always being urbane,
With boot and spur —
No, Sir!

To be that light
Can't be quite right . . ."
Soon a third comes on.
Maybe he'll be the one.

Shepherd's Pouch and Sheep's Yarrow

"Shepherd's Pouch, wee Shepherd's Pouch,
Come to my sheep meadow couch.
Bring your little water-pouch too,
Dog and shepherd, both of you!

Let me pasture all your sheep;
Every one for you I'll keep,
Every black and every white.
Where's your lunch? Let's have a bite!

Now with me there's lots of food,
Sheaves aripening sweet and good,
Nice new bread for us to eat —
Life with me will be complete!"

"Shepherd's Pouch," the sheep-dog barks,
"To what she says you should not hark!
Deep in the meadow, just you and I,
Will find fresh grass to pasture by!"

The Journey of Mourning Cloak

Once upon a time there was a King who was always sad. Gloomy and melancholy, he sat upon his throne, and his name was Mourning Cloak. But because he could never be happy, his people deposed him. He lost his kingdom and had to flee.

On the shore the Sailor waited for him with his ship. The King went on board and they sailed far out into the wide ocean. They hoped to find a happier land, and they trusted their ship to the wind. The wind blew the ship among high waves. Silvery dragonflies frolicked around the mast, and blue butterflies lit on the rope, taking a rest from their flight.

The King thought of his misfortune and wept. On his concertina the Soloist played beautiful melodies to the roaring of the wind. But that only made the King grow sadder. Then a terrible storm came up, and the ship threatened to sink.

"If you do not cast away your sorrow and care, we are lost," said the Sailor. Then there came an inner light into the heart of the King — he threw his sorrow and care into the sea and vowed to be happy and cheerful from then on.

And the storm died down, the water grew calm — the ship was saved.

In the distance there rose to view the happy shore which the Sailor had sought, and where they now could land.

Peony

Peony sits on a bed of grass
With her toddlers on her knee;
Red petals on the ground are cast,
All strewn about those three.

The grassy Skinnystalks grow there
And craftily watch them all;
They reach out of hiding into the air,
Wherever the petals fall.

They all would like to catch a leaf,
But a leaf not all could find;
Like butterflies, some leaves fly off
To wander in the wind.

The little ones look on with glee
Till baby wraps come away,
And they will leave their mother's knee
To have their fun in May.

The Admiral and His Fleet

The Admiral stood on the ocean shore and said, "Why am I called an Admiral if I am not really an Admiral and have no fleet?" His friends, the Bluelets, the Whitelets, and the Blacklings, agreed with him. Well, the Beetles went right to work and hauled into the water, the dry leaves which lay on the shore. These were their ships. The Whitelets and the Blacklings sat in the ships, and they were sails and rudders.

For the Admiral, however, a very large leaf was used, a rudder was fastened to it, many oars were carved, and a mast was mounted with tackle and Butterfly sails; Beetle rowers and a Beetle band took their places. The Admiral and his officers went aboard the ship. The band began to play. The wind blew and the fleet put out to sea. Now he had become a proper Admiral.

Petunia, Betony, Begonia

Begonia's awake in her house of glass;
Outside the sun is climbing fast.
"Come out with us, come out, come out!
It's late for you to be lying about."

"The sun for me shines just as fair
As he can do for you out there!
Why do you tap on my window to come?
I am just as happy here at home.

In my house so full of light
The rain can never make me wet.
The wind can't ruffle up my dress —
Leave me alone where I like it best!"

The Cockfight

"Come on, green Cockscomb, noisy clown!
What will you do with that golden crown?"

"You insolent red Cockscomb, best
Not try to make something out of my crest!"

'Oho, you glaucous Beak-for-bite,
Forget the bluster, come and fight!"

Pick, peck, and whack, at neck and all —
The little green one was too small.

The red one got him, back of the neck,
And that was the end of the puny green chick.

The Eagle Fern, the Viper's Bugloss,
Pitied the poor little bird, alas!

Heart's Tongue and Chamois Beard so brave,
Bear's Moss and Goat Beard praised his nerve.

Milkweed, Foxtail, and Wild Bear Thistle
Felt that Fate too soon blew the whistle.

The Storkbeaks seated high on the hill
Clapped their applause with the point of the bill.

Kitten's Paw became very sad,
And Rabbit's Mouth got downright mad.

But big old Dandelion cried,
"Why are you all on this Cockscomb's side?"

"He was just too weak and just too small,
He should have acted a bit less tall!"

The Inn in the Forest

On a hot summer day when all the Butterflies were busy in the forest and on the meadow seeking honey, a violent thunder shower suddenly unloaded. It was impossible to reach home, and all the Butterflies took refuge in a Forest Inn.

That was an old cardboard box where a House Mother lived. She had many pupae in her care and served refreshing juices to drink.

"Welcome," she said, greeting the guests who came tumbling in: Copperluck, the beautiful Blue Peacock, and the Lady Icebird. Sand Eye, Buckeye, and several Whitelets were already there. The first heavy raindrops fell. The lightning flashed and thunder rolled. Little Sulpher White fainted from fright. "Quick! A glass of Tree Potion!" called good Mrs. Cabbage Butterfly, and the House Mother brought it fast. It poured torrents. Then cries for help came from the roof. Birchtip Butterfly had been carried along by the heavy rain and had remained stuck to the roof by his wings. Always ready to help, Wood Porter got him down with his fork and brought him inside where he soon recovered.

New guests came rushing in, dripping wet. "O, my beautiful dress, my beautiful dress!" they moaned. The Emperor's Coat came with Lady Silver Streak, whose wings had been damaged by the storm, and Checkerspot and Alpine Butterfly, who had gotten lost. Then there was a lot of work for House Mother, for each one needed refreshment. But everything came out fine, and the Butterflies stayed in the Forest Inn until the storm was over.

Alpine Flowers

Edelweiss on the hill,
So close to the sky,
Watch the clouds fill
And slowly sail by;
Gaze down the slope
Where other flowers sleep;
Hear the birds chant;
Breathe in the scent . . .
The flower listens still
For the echoes to call.

Small Alpine rose,
Sing Heidi ridei!
With staff and shoes
Alpen Bells dance by.
Each hat with a bell
Is under a spell.
They dance in a ring,
In groups take a fling,
Or else in twos,
As the spell may choose.

Edelweiss smiles
For miles and miles.
The evening creeps
On them from far,
And the flowers sleep
In care of a star.

The Caterpillar Garden

Mr. Ermine had a Caterpillar Garden, which was his greatest joy. Every morning before breakfast he visited it and was especially pleased by the beautiful colors of these creatures, by the blue and black ribbons which ran straight or slanting across their backs, by the red and white polka-dots, the eyes, rings, and spots, by their feelers and beards, and by their good appetites. Water Nymph had just brought their food, something different for each one: milkweed for Milkweed Caterpillar, potato tops for Death's Head Caterpillar, whilst Copper Caterpillar got blackthorn leaves, Swallowtail Caterpillar got carrot leaves, Pear Spinner, pear tree leaves, and Vine Hawkmoth just bedstraw. Then she sprinkled each one with fresh water and said, "Hearty appetite!" Dung Beetle, however, did his work silently. "Does it taste good?" Mr. Ermine asked his Caterpillars. They all nodded their heads and went right on eating greedily, for with the exception of Death's Head Caterpillar they couldn't talk. Death's Head Caterpillar had a voice and whispered in her neighbor's ear, "Today it still tastes good and tomorrow it will, too, but the day after tomorrow we must go away." Water Nymph heard this and told Mr. Ermine. He did not want to lose his beautiful Caterpillars. He ordered the garden gate to be closed tightly at night and the garden to be strictly watched. Nevertheless, on the third day all the Caterpillars disappeared — they had crawled under the dry leaves and into the ground, in order to be changed into Butterflies and Mr. Ermine no longer had a Caterpillar Garden.

Ground Ivy and Creeping Bugle

At the Pharmacy Ground Ivy,
Sir Creeping Bugle appears,
Crawling on his hands and knees
And loud with moans and tears.

"O Pharmacist Ground Ivy!
I am sick. You must have a cure.
As you must see, I can scarcely walk,
The pain is everywhere."

The pharmacist now clears his throat:
"Sure, I can fix your trouble,
For I have berries and herbs and roots
That go to work on the double."

"For example, I have Ground Ivy tea
And Camomile and Bogbean,
Elderberry, Walmeister and bedstraw,
If you feel real thirsty and mean."

I have Ribgrass here for injured skin,
Horsetail to cool the blood;
And then there's Thousandguilden tea —
For the stomach that's very good.

Eyebright is excellent for the eyes,
And Strawflower for the gout;
And always I find a pine-needle bath
Brings comfort without a doubt."

Sir Creeping Bugle drinks five cups of tea,
And he sweats and he sweats. O Jiminy!

Creeping Bugle praises all this skill,
And then he pauses and says, "Er, well —

A cold bath right after one that is hot
Makes all his crooked limbs grow straight;

Mr. Ground Ivy, your bill must be large?"
"Seven guilders only is my charge."

And, believe it or not, from this very hour,
He's healthy once again for sure.

"So kind of you, Sir, and thanks a million.
It happens I don't have any guildern,

But just because you've been so nice,
I'll come back again for your advice."

The Caterpillar Circus

In his most beautiful coat the Bear Trainer came into the cage, swung his staff, and shouted, "Hee, la, la, la, la, la, up!"

The Bear Caterpillar stood up and danced on his hind legs. High above on a perch sat the Owl Butterflies who made magic music so that Forked Tail Caterpillar began to perform on the high wire. While he was doing that, he made a face like a dragon and the red threads on his forked tail trembled so much that everyone was afraid. Looper looped up to him in great arches and Camelid Caterpillar, too. Brush-Maker with his bundles of bristles acted as if he were entranced by the music and hurried to climb the pole. Only Thistle-Butterfly Caterpillar was stubborn. She writhed on the ground and stretched her prickles in all directions.

Astonished and amazed, the spectators stood by the cage, clapped and shouted, "Da capo, da capo! More, more!" The Bear Trainer bowed, thanked them for their applause, and allowed the act to be performed again. Then he shouted, "Ho, la, la, la, la, down!" The music grew silent; the Caterpillars stopped dancing and ran happily to their stalls. Only Brush-Maker had to brush the coat of the Bear Trainer once more. That was the end of the performance.

Solomon's Seal

What are the three king's daughters doing in the wood?
Are they wandering there just to rest in the shade?
Ah no! Ah no!
To the evil magician within it is they go.

There is a Sorcerer, deep in the forest drear;
He is very old and he is covered with hair:
Stuck fast in the earth, as if they had rooted his heel,
Because he once had stolen King Solomon's seal.

"What do you three king's daughters want of me?"
They hear and are moved to shudder at all they see.
"Trusting and daring, into this woods we go,
Because 'tis the future that we from you would know."

"I know,' quoth the Sorcerer, "you think of whom you'll wed.
The ones who will woo you must not be far," he said.
"I give unto each one now this chain of gold,
With which to bind your sweethearts — and to hold.

Your lover will not see it, will be blind to the chain;
But watch and be mindful it does not break in twain;
For if it does, a beetle of emerald will gnaw
Your heart away unseen ere you can withdraw."

Whereon, the compact tied between those four,
It thundered, it rumbled, the earth split with a roar;
And the Sorcerer, on that spot, forlorn beyond belief,
Sank down, while the little bells shook on the leaf.

Moonlit Night

When it gets dark in the forest, the Night Butterflies awaken. They go around between the bushes, looking with their glowing eyes for playmates, and when they have found them, they dance through the air like mad and sit down on the flowers to drink honey; with a long proboscis they drink it in flight from flower blossoms. Then they settle on the forest ground, take pleasure walks in the shadows of the bushes, and breathe in the sharp smell of the earth which rises everywhere. Then the Moon comes up behind the forest and looks over the quiet world with its silvery pale face.

Tut, tut, tut sounds from the distance. That's Stag Beetle. He approaches with heavy steps so that big Night Peacock Eye and Goat Moth are afraid and hide. Anxiously, the Black Arches fly up and down, and the Owl Butterflies flutter back and forth with sorrowful cries.

"Let him go past," whispers Night Peacock Eye to Goat Moth. "He is much stronger than we are; he would kill us." The crunching and gnashing of the Terrible Beetle dies away. The forest is again free for the Butterflies with their silky gleam.

The Moon rises higher and higher and draws a great arc across the entire sky.

The Day comes and the Night Butterflies go to sleep.

Clematis

High on the trellis the vine is blooming,
The shape of its blossom compelling.
I hear the evening breezes tuning
A melody gradually swelling.

Clematis white, clematis blue,
In the luminous summer night,
Have given a musical interview
In the garden for my delight.

The type face in this book is Antique Olive and was set by Triple ''T'' Typographers, El Cajon, California.

Printed by Inter-Collegiate Press
Shawnee Mission, Kansas